THE CURSED REFLECTION

INDU DIXIT

To my younger self, who first imagined this story and gave
it life on the page. I never thought I'd see it published, but
here we are. This book is for you, and I hope you'd be
proud of how far it's come.

Contents

Contents

Acknowledgements

Thank you to everyone who reads this story. I hope it brings you as much enjoyment as I had in creating it.

Preface

What follows is a tale of discovery, mystery, and, yes, a bit of terror. It explores the darker side of human (or in this case, Lamia's) curiosity, where sometimes the answers we find are ones we may wish had remained hidden. As you step into this world, remember—sometimes, knowing too much can be the scariest thing of all.

Foreword

Thank you for picking up this story.
It is a good story
but
If it makes you pause, look over your shoulder, or
wonder just a little more about the unknown,
THEN IT HAS DONE ITS JOB

Prologue

The night Lamia was born, the storm was unlike any other. The sky cracked open with thunder, and the wind howled through the village, as if the world itself was screaming. Her mother died giving birth, leaving Lamia alone in the dark, cold world.

The villagers whispered that her birth had caused the storm—that she was cursed from the start. And as Lamia grew, strange things began to happen around her. Shadows seemed to follow her, and her reflection in the mirror looked... wrong.

Little did she know, the storm wasn't the only thing she had brought into the world. And as she would soon learn, some things are not just in your reflection—they're part of you.

The Stormy Birth

Lamia's birth was shadowed by darkness from the very start. The night she entered the world, a storm like no other shook the village. The storm was fierce—angry even. Thunder shattered the night air with booming cracks, each one louder than the last, as if the sky itself was ripping apart. Lightning was piercing through the clouds, briefly turning night to day, only to plunge the world back into darkness seconds later. Rain fell in sheets, pounding against rooftops and flooding the narrow, muddy streets, creating large streams of water that rushed down the village's slopes and back toward the sea.

On the night Lamia was born, the sky was wild and fierce, her mother, a kind young woman, gave birth in a small cottage, whispering her love to her baby girl before passing away with a gentle smile.

When the sun finally rose, the storm calmed, and mist rolled in, covering the village in a soft blanket of fog. Inside the cottage, Lamia lay bundled in warm blankets her mother had left for her. The villagers whispered to each other, still shaken by the night's strange events. Some of them were afraid and whispered to each other that Lamia's birth had brought the storm. "Is she a cursed child?" they wondered, while others thought she might be special in a magical way.

As Lamia grew, she often felt the stares and heard the whispers, but she also sensed something strong inside her, like a spark. She didn't know what it meant, but she felt deep down that she had a purpose—a story to live that was beginning. And though she was different, she was ready to find out just what that meant. Even on the darkest night, Lamia knew there was always a light to guide her forward, and she was determined to follow it. She lived the first few years of her childhood just like this.

A Life of Shadows

Lamia's new life began on a cold, gray morning as she was taken from the cozy warmth of her mother's cottage to live with her aunt in a small, shadowy cottage at the edge of the village. As she stood on the ground at the entrance to her new home, the memories of her mother's love flooded her mind. Elara had filled their cottage with laughter, stories, and bright flowers, but now Lamia faced an unfamiliar place that felt cold and uninviting. The walls were dark and bare, and the air hung heavy with an unsettling silence.

Her aunt, a stern woman with a face like a storm cloud, looked down at her with disapproval. The moment Lamia entered the cottage, she sensed that her aunt would not offer her the warmth and comfort she had once known. Her aunt never spoke of her mother, choosing instead to focus on her chores and her own daily life. Lamia felt invisible, like a ghost drifting through the shadows of the cottage, where the only sounds were the creaking of the floorboards and the distant howling of the wind outside.

Days turned into weeks, and Lamia's life settled into an ever-repeating routine. She woke up before dawn, her aunt's voice cutting through the silence as she demanded Lamia fetch water from the well or clean the dusty corners of the cottage. Each task felt worse every time, and her aunt's constant frown seemed to darken the already dim house. Lamia longed for the care and love her mother would have given her, a caretaker, who would have praised her efforts with gentle words and bright smiles.

As the villagers went about their daily routines, they often cast fearful glances in Lamia's direction. Whispers followed her like a shadow, carrying tales of curses and misfortune. "She's just like her mother," they murmured (even though that wasn't the case at all), "bringing storms and sorrow wherever she goes." The children in the village, taught to fear the unknown, began to avoid her, exchanging laughter for mocking glances. Lamia's heart sank each time she saw a group of children playing, their giggles ringing out like distant music, reminding her of the happiness that seemed forever out of reach.

Feeling the weight of her isolation, Lamia often found comfort in the small garden behind the cottage. It was a wild, tangled place, filled with weeds and thorny brambles. Yet, in that garden, she felt a connection to her mother. Elara had loved flowers, nurturing them with care and telling Lamia tales of their magic. Lamia would often talk to the flowers as if they could hear her, sharing her hopes and dreams with the daisies and sunflowers, imagining they were her friends.

In her loneliness, Lamia began to notice strange occurrences around her. One afternoon, as she sat among the flowers, she felt a gentle breeze brush against her face. To her astonishment, the flowers began to sway and dance as if they were responding to her presence. She giggled, thinking it must be a trick of the wind, but deep down, she felt a flicker of something magical within her. It was as if the earth was alive, and somehow, she was a part of it.

One evening, while helping her aunt prepare dinner, Lamia's mind wandered to the forest she could see in the distance. The tall trees stood like guardians, whispering secrets to one another. With a sudden rush of determination, Lamia decided she would explore that forest only to feel a sense of belonging again.

The next day, when her aunt was too busy scolding her for a minor mistake in the kitchen, Lamia seized the opportunity to slip away. As she entered the forest, a sense of freedom came over her. The sunlight streamed through the leaves, creating a shimmering blanket of light that made her heart race with excitement. She ventured deeper, following the sound of rustling leaves and distant birdsong.

Lamia felt as if she were stepping into a different world, one filled with magic and wonder. The air was fragrant with the scent of pine and wildflowers, and she could hear the soft babble of a stream nearby. Every step she took brought her closer to a sense of belonging, and she imagined her mother walking beside her, guiding her through the forest.

As she wandered, she encountered curious animals—squirrels chattering in the trees, rabbits peeking from behind bushes, and even a family of deer grazing in a sunlit clearing. To her surprise, they seemed unafraid of her presence, approaching her with a gentle curiosity. Lamia knelt down, reaching out a hand, and to her delight, a small rabbit hopped closer, sniffing her fingers. "You're not afraid of me, are you?" she whispered, feeling a warmth in her heart.

With each passing day, Lamia continued to explore the forest, discovering secret glades and hidden streams. She felt a connection with the creatures she met, often spending hours watching the animals play and chase each other. The loneliness that had once clung to her began to lift, replaced by a sense of purpose and belonging among the trees.

Yet, the whispers of the villagers remained. Whenever she returned home, she could feel their stares, as if they were trying to uncover secret life. Children would point and whisper, their eyes wide with fear, as they turned away from her. One day, as Lamia gathered wildflowers to brighten her aunt's gloomy cottage, a group of children threw stones at her, laughing as they called her names.

"Cursed child! You'll bring the storms!" one boy shouted, his words scarring, Lamia felt tears prick in her eyes as she ran from the village, her heart heavy with sadness. She wanted to shout back, to tell them that she was not cursed, but special, just like her mother had been. But the words stuck in her throat, and all she could do was escape into the comforting embrace of the forest.

In the depths of the woods, she found a hidden a narrow valley deep in the mountains, a magical place where the sun shone brightly and the air was sweet with the scent of blooming flowers. It was here that Lamia felt the weight of the world lift from her shoulders. She danced among the flowers, twirling and spinning, letting her laughter echo through the trees. In that moment, she was free—a wild spirit, unbound by the fears of the villagers.

One day, as she lay in the grass, gazing up at the sky, she felt a strange sensation wash over her. It was as if the forest was alive, responding to her thoughts and feelings. The leaves rustled softly, and she could swear she heard her mother's voice in the breeze. "You are not alone, my dear," it seemed to say. "You are part of the magic of this world."

Filled with a sense of purpose, Lamia began to collect treasures from the forest. She gathered feathers, shiny stones, and delicate flowers, creating a small altar in the glen where she could honor her mother's memory. Each item held a story, a connection to her past, and a promise for the future. As she arranged them, she felt a surge of energy, as if the forest was blessing her with its magic.

Yet, as much as she found comfort in her secret life, Lamia could not escape the shadow of her aunt's neglect. Returning to the cottage each evening was a stark reminder of her loneliness. Her aunt would often scold her for being out too late, her sharp words cutting through the air like thorns. Lamia learned to keep her adventures a secret, hiding her treasures beneath loose floorboards and in hidden corners of her room.

One stormy night, as thunder rumbled in the distance, Lamia's aunt summoned her to the kitchen. "You must

learn to help around the house," she snapped, her voice
harsh. "You can't go running off to play in the woods like a
wild animal. People are talking about you."

Lamia felt a knot tighten in her stomach. "But I'm not a
wild animal! I'm just exploring!" she protested, but her
aunt dismissed her words with a wave of her hand.
"Enough! You're a burden, and your mother's foolishness
has brought nothing but trouble. Do you think I want to
raise a cursed child?"

Lamia's heart sank. Her aunt's words felt like icy daggers
piercing her soul, leaving her breathless with hurt. As she
turned away, tears streaming down her cheeks, she vowed
to herself that she would not let her aunt's harshness
define her. She would uncover the truth about her mother
and the magic that seemed to flow through her veins.

In the days that followed, Lamia felt a growing
determination to embrace her uniqueness. She spent
more time in the forest, deepening her bond with nature
and honing her newfound abilities. The more she
explored, the more she realized that she had a connection
to the world around her, a power that set her apart.
Flowers bloomed in her presence, and she found herself
communicating with animals in ways she had never
thought possible.

One afternoon, while sitting beneath the enchanted oak,
Lamia closed her eyes and let her thoughts drift. Suddenly,
she felt a warm energy enveloping her. It was as if the tree
was responding to her heart, wrapping her in a cocoon of

love and light. She felt her mother's spirit surrounding her, whispering words of encouragement and strength. "You are not cursed, dear Lamia," the voice echoed softly. "You are a protector of this land, a keeper of magic."

The realization filled her with hope. Lamia opened her eyes, a renewed sense of purpose blossoming within her. She knew that her journey was just beginning, and she was ready to face the challenges ahead. With each passing day, she grew stronger and more confident, embracing her identity as a child of magic, a child of the forest.

As she returned home that evening, Lamia felt a surge of courage coursing through her veins. She would no longer allow her aunt's words to hold her back. With every step, she promised to uncover the truth about her mother and the legacy that awaited her. No longer would she hide in the shadows—she was ready to shine.

Lamia stood tall as she approached the cottage, a spark of determination lighting her heart. She would prove to everyone, including herself, that she was special. She would embrace her destiny and uncover the magic within.

Lamia stood tall as she approached the cottage, a spark of determination lighting her heart. She would prove to everyone, including herself, that she was special. She would embrace her destiny and uncover the magic within.

The Mirror's Call

As Lamia stepped into her teenage years, the world around her seemed to transform, and so did she. The familiar landscape of her childhood home felt both comforting and stifling. Her once-beloved toys were gathering dust in the corner, the stories that used to ignite her imagination now faded like old photographs. It was during one of these restless afternoons, when the weight of expectation pressed heavily on her shoulders, that she stumbled upon her mother's old mirror hidden in the attic.

The attic was a labyrinth of forgotten treasures and dusty memories, a place she rarely visited. Sunlight filtered through a grimy window, casting ethereal beams of light that danced across the wooden floor. As she moved through the cobwebs, her heart quickened at the sight of the mirror. Its ornate frame was intricately carved with twisting vines and figures that seemed to dance in the light. The glass was slightly fogged, but she could still make out her reflection.

Drawn to its haunting beauty, Lamia approached, her fingers brushing against the cool, glass surface. For a moment, she was mesmerized by the way the light caught the reflections, creating a shimmering effect that felt almost alive. The mirror seemed to pulse with a strange energy as if it were calling her closer. As she gazed deeper, she felt an inexplicable pull, as if the mirror was calling her name in a whisper only she could hear.

Every day after that, Lamia found herself returning to the attic, enchanted by the mirror's perplexing presence. She would sit cross-legged on the dusty floor, entranced by the reflections that seemed to swirl within the glass. At first, it was just her own image staring back, but soon, she noticed subtle shifts—a flicker of movement at the edges of her vision, shadows that seemed to dance just beyond the frame. The mirror held a dark faination that grew stronger with each passing day.

Her fascination soon turned into an obsession. Lamia spent hours before the mirror, sharing her secrets and dreams, pouring out her heart as if the glass could somehow absorb her feelings. She confided in it about her hopes for the future, her fears of growing up, and the loneliness that often crept into her life like an unwelcome guest. The mirror seemed to respond in its own way, offering a silent companionship that was both comforting and unnerving.

As she explored the attic further, she uncovered forgotten trinkets of her mother's past—a silver locket, old photographs, and letters filled with swirling, elegant handwriting. Each item told a fragment of a story Lamia yearned to piece together. But the mirror was different; it felt alive, pulsating with an energy that beckoned her to unveil its mysteries.

One stormy evening, as rain lashed against the attic window, Lamia sat before the mirror, its surface shining like a darkened sea. Thunder rumbled in the distance, and the shadows in the room stretched and flickered like living beings. She closed her eyes, allowing the sounds of the storm to fade into the background, and whispered her mother's name. As she did, she felt a chill sweep through the room, and when she opened her eyes, the mirror's surface had transformed.

Instead of her reflection, she saw a blurred figure standing in a dimly lit room. The figure wore an old-fashioned dress, the fabric flowing like mist, and the air around it shimmered as if caught between worlds. Lamia's heart raced as she leaned closer, her breath fogging the surface. "Mother?" she called, her voice trembling.

But the figure did not respond. Instead, it pointed toward something hidden in the shadows behind it. Lamia felt a surge of curiosity and fear, as if the mirror was revealing a secret that had been buried for too long. She reached out, her fingertips grazing the surface, and in that instant, the world around her seemed to dissolve.

Suddenly, she was standing in the room the figure inhabited. The air was thick with an eerie silence, and the walls were adorned with paintings of landscapes she had never seen. The light was dim, casting elongated shadows that danced along the walls. In the center of the room stood the figure—her mother, or what she thought was her mother—facing away, her hair cascading like a waterfall of darkness.

"Why did you leave?" Lamia's voice echoed in the stillness, but there was no answer. The figure turned slowly, and

Lamia felt a jolt of recognition mingled with terror. The face was familiar yet foreign, an older version of her mother with eyes that glinted with unspoken sorrow.

"Lamia..." the figure began, her voice a mere whisper against the backdrop of the storm, but before she could finish, the scene flickered, the colors draining away like water through a sieve. Lamia gasped, the connection severed, and she found herself back in the attic, heart pounding, her mind racing with questions.

What had she seen? Had it been a glimpse into her mother's past, or something darker that lingered within the mirror? The boundaries of reality blurred as Lamia's obsession deepened, drawing her into a web of secrets woven into her family's history. She felt compelled to uncover more, as if the mirror was a bridge between her world and the secrets of her mother's past.

With each return to the mirror, Lamia found herself more and more entangled in its mysteries. The mirror began to show her fleeting images—snapshots of moments that felt painfully familiar yet utterly foreign. A young woman dancing in a moonlit garden, laughter echoing through the night; a darkened hallway lined with portraits that seemed to watch her with knowing eyes. Each image tugged at her heart, igniting a longing to understand the woman her mother once was, and the reasons behind the whispers that surrounded her.

One fateful night, unable to resist the mirror's call, Lamia resolved to confront whatever lay beyond its surface. She gathered her courage, fueled by the questions that swirled in her mind. As she stood before the mirror, her reflection seemed to shimmer, "Show me," she whispered, her voice barely audible over the howling wind.

The glass rippled like water, and suddenly, she was pulled into a vivid dreamscape. The room before her was transformed—a lavish ballroom filled with elegantly dressed figures dancing under a crystal chandelier. The music went on, and the scent of blooming roses filled the air. Lamia's heart raced as she realized she was seeing a memory, one that belonged to her mother.

In the midst of the revelry, she spotted the figure from before—her mother, radiating beauty and grace. Yet there was a sadness in her eyes that contrasted sharply with the joy around her. Lamia felt a wave of emotions wash over her, empathy intertwining with confusion. She reached out, desperate to bridge the gap, to understand the sorrow that clung to her mother even in the midst of happiness.

"Mother!" she called, but the words were lost in the thrumming music. The figures danced around her, oblivious to her presence, as if she were a ghost haunting the edges of their joy. Lamia searched for a way to connect, to break through the veil of time, but the harder she tried, the more elusive her mother became.

Just then, the music shifted, becoming more somber, the dancers slowing to a halt. A shadow fell across the room, darkening the once vibrant atmosphere. The laughter faded, replaced by whispers that echoed with malice.

Lamia felt the cold grip of fear wrapping around her heart as she recognized the malevolent presence that had been lurking behind her mother all along.

Suddenly, the ballroom dissolved into chaos. Figures swirled into shadows, and the once-vibrant colors bled into darkness. Lamia screamed, reaching for her mother, but the figure was pulled away, disappearing into the void. "No!" Lamia cried, but her voice was swallowed by the encroaching darkness.

In a blinding flash, she found herself back in the attic, gasping for breath, the mirror now a mere reflection of her frightened face. The comforting weight of the attic was gone, replaced by an oppressive silence that settled heavily on her shoulders. The storm outside had intensified, thunder rumbling ominously as if responding to her terror.

Lamia knew she had touched something far more profound and dangerous than she had anticipated. The mirror was not merely a reflection of her mother's past; it was a conduit to the darker forces that had shaped her family's history. She felt a deep sense of dread settling in her stomach as she pieced together the fragments of what she had seen. Her mother's sadness, the shadow that loomed over her happiness—it was all connected, woven into the very fabric of the mirror.

What had begun as a simple curiosity now morphed into a haunting journey that threatened to consume her. Lamia understood that she had to uncover the truth behind the mirror's call before it pulled her too deeply into the shadows. With determination igniting her spirit, she resolved to confront the secrets of her past, even if it meant facing the darkness that lurked within.

As she stepped away from the mirror, she cast one last glance at its surface. For the first time, she felt the weight of her own reflection staring back at her, a mixture of fear and resolve shining in her eyes. The journey ahead would be perilous, but Lamia was ready to unearth the secrets that lay hidden within the glass—a journey that would change her life forever.

The Cracked Reflection

As Lamia grew older, the strange pull of the mirror grew stronger, each year amplifying its call until it became something undeniable. What had once been simple curiosity turned into an insistent, almost magnetic force. The mirror had always been there, in the corner of the attic, gathering dust. But over time, Lamia could feel it watching her, as if it had a presence, a life of its own. She didn't understand it, but there was no denying that every time she passed by it, her gaze would be drawn to it. It felt different, more than just a reflection, more than just a piece of glass. It felt like a doorway to something she couldn't quite grasp, a doorway that was slowly pulling her in.

At first, she told herself it was nothing. A strange trick of light. A figment of her imagination. After all, mirrors were just mirrors, weren't they? But the more she stared, the more she saw. The reflections weren't always right. Sometimes, her face in the mirror seemed too distant, too cold. Other times, it seemed to change, twisting slightly, as though the glass itself was alive. It was subtle at first, the changes so small that she almost convinced herself she was imagining them. But soon, she couldn't ignore it. There was something off about the way her reflection moved—how it lingered just a fraction too long when she turned her head, or how it smiled when her own lips remained still. It made her heart race, made her question if her eyes were playing tricks on her, or if the mirror was showing her something darker.

She could feel the mirror's pull in her bones. It was as if the glass was calling her name, whispering things she couldn't quite hear. At first, it was faint, like a soft hum in the background of her thoughts. But over time, the whispers became louder, clearer. They were not words she could understand, but they were persistent, and they beckoned her, like a siren's song. Every day, Lamia found herself standing in front of it, staring into the glass, wondering what secrets it held. She didn't understand why it fascinated her so much, but she couldn't stay away.

There were days when she would stand in front of the mirror for hours, just watching, waiting for something to happen. It was as though the mirror held a promise, a promise that it would reveal its secrets to her, but only if she was patient enough to wait for them. And so, she did. She waited, watching as her reflection slowly twisted and warped before her eyes. Sometimes, she thought she saw her mother's face in the mirror, pale and sad, like a ghost trapped in the glass. Other times, she thought she saw someone else—someone she didn't recognize, someone who seemed to be watching her from the other side of the glass.

But it was on her sixteenth birthday that everything changed.

The wind howled outside, rattling the windows, as a storm brewed in the distance. Lamia had always loved storms, the way the air seemed to crackle with energy, the way the thunder rumbled in her chest, like the world was alive and breathing. But tonight was different. Tonight, it was as if the storm outside mirrored the chaos inside her heart. There was something heavy in the air, something electric, as if the world was holding its breath, waiting for something to happen.

She stood in front of the mirror, feeling its pull more intensely than ever before. The storm outside seemed to press against the walls of the house, the wind howling and the rain beating down like a thousand tiny fists. Lamia's heart raced, not out of fear, but out of something else—something she couldn't name. She knew she had to face the mirror tonight. She didn't know why, but it felt like the moment had arrived. It felt like the mirror had been waiting for her, waiting for this very night to reveal its secrets.

Her hand trembled as she reached out toward the glass, her fingers brushing lightly against the surface. The second her skin made contact, everything shifted. The mirror rippled, like water disturbed by a stone. The glass seemed to come alive, shifting and warping before her eyes. Lamia gasped, pulling her hand away in shock, but it was too late. A sharp, searing pain shot through her chest, and she felt her heart stop for a brief moment, as if the world itself had paused in that instant.

She staggered backward, her breath catching in her throat, and her eyes locked onto her reflection. But when she looked again, something was wrong. Her reflection was gone. It wasn't there anymore.

Instead, there was something else.

Where her reflection had been, there was now a twisted version of herself. Her face was pale—pale to the point of being ghostly. Her eyes were deep, hollowed-out pits of darkness, like there was nothing inside them. The smile on her face was twisted, stretched too wide, too unnatural. It wasn't her smile. It couldn't be. It was something darker, something wrong. Lamia's pulse raced, a wave of cold fear washing over her. Her reflection—her own reflection—was staring at her, grinning with that unsettling, twisted smile. But it wasn't smiling at her in the way she knew. It was smiling at something else, something she couldn't see, something beyond her.

"What... What is this?" Lamia whispered, her voice trembling. She couldn't breathe. Her head spun, her vision blurred, but she couldn't tear her eyes away from the mirror. The twisted reflection in the glass didn't move. It just stood there, smiling, watching her.

She stumbled back, her legs giving way beneath her. The storm outside seemed to rage louder, as if the world itself was screaming along with her. Lamia's hands shook as she reached out toward the mirror, as if she could somehow touch her reflection, as if doing so might make it all go away. But when she pressed her hand to the glass, the twisted reflection's hand moved, as if it were mirroring her every move. The glass felt cold, colder than she had ever felt before. It was like pressing her hand to ice, but the cold was seeping deeper, into her very bones.

The figure in the mirror spoke then. It was her voice, but twisted, distorted, like a faint echo from the deepest parts of her mind.

"Lamia," the voice whispered, its tone soft but chilling. "You've been waiting for me."

Her heart stopped. Her breath caught in her throat. How did it know her name? How did it know she had been waiting for this moment, for this truth to reveal itself? She had always known something was wrong, always felt there was something hidden beneath the surface of the mirror, but she never imagined this. Never imagined this version of herself staring back at her, this distorted, hollow version.

"No," Lamia whispered, shaking her head. "This isn't real. It can't be real."

But the figure in the mirror only smiled wider, its smile stretching impossibly wide, like it could reach all the way across the glass. "Oh, it's real, Lamia," it said, its voice sweet but thick with something darker. "You've always known I was here. You just didn't want to see."

The storm outside exploded in a flash of lightning. The wind howled like a wild animal, rattling the walls. Lamia's pulse raced, her body frozen in place as the figure in the mirror reached out, pressing its hand against the glass. Lamia's hand moved, almost as if it had a mind of its own, as it reached out to meet the figure's cold, outstretched fingers.

When their hands touched the glass, Lamia felt a jolt run through her, a shock that made her whole body tremble. The air around her turned icy, and her lungs felt as if they had frozen. She could barely breathe, barely think. The storm outside became deafening, the thunder so loud it shook the house. The mirror cracked then, a jagged line slicing through the glass, but the figure didn't move. It stayed there, staring at her, smiling that same, twisted smile.

"You can't hide from me anymore, Lamia," the figure whispered, its voice sending chills down her spine.

Lamia gasped, stumbling back from the mirror as the figure vanished, leaving only the jagged crack in the glass as a reminder of what she had seen. The storm raged on outside, but inside, all was quiet. Lamia stood there, her heart pounding, her body frozen in fear. She had seen the truth now, the truth that had been hidden behind the mirror all along. And there was no turning back.

The Dream of Hollow Manor

That night, Lamia felt the weight of the world on her shoulders as she drifted into a deep and restless sleep. Her mind, often filled with confusing thoughts and strange desires, began to lose touch with reality, slipping into a place that was both strange and familiar. She was no longer lying in her small, quiet bedroom. The soft hum of her usual surroundings faded into the background as she found herself standing in the middle of a massive, cold hall.

The air was heavy with an eerie stillness, thick as if it had not moved for years, perhaps even centuries. Her breath came out in small, anxious clouds that seemed to hang in the air longer than they should have, refusing to fade away. The grand hall was not at all like her home, or any place she had ever seen before. It felt ancient, forgotten by time itself. The high ceiling stretched so far above her, out of sight, and the walls, made of dark, weathered stone, felt as if they were pressing in on her. The place was enormous, but the silence that filled it made it seem even larger, like it was swallowing her up bit by bit, inch by inch.

She stood in awe, her eyes scanning the room as she tried to understand where she was and how she had arrived here. Everything was foreign, yet the feeling of being watched, being observed from all corners, was something she could not shake. The hall was lined with portraits, but not just any portraits. These portraits were strange. The children depicted in the paintings had eyes so empty, so hollow, that it felt like they were looking straight through her. Their expressions were solemn and sad, but there was something deeper there, something that made Lamia's stomach tighten with fear. The longer she stared at the painted faces, the more it seemed like they were slowly starting to follow her, their eyes moving in her direction, tracking her every step.

Lamia's heart beat faster. She could feel their gaze, cold and heavy, pressing down on her from all sides. They whispered to her, their voices barely audible but unmistakable. At first, it was a soft murmur, barely a whisper, but the longer she stood there, the louder the voices became, until they surrounded her, echoing in her mind.

"Lamia..."

Her name. She heard it over and over again, faint, distant, like a chant drifting through the air. Each time the whispers called her, they seemed to draw her in, pulling her closer to the center of the hall. Lamia felt an overwhelming urge to answer, to move toward them, but her feet felt frozen, unwilling to obey. The whispers became louder, more insistent, growing into a chorus of voices that filled her ears, spinning her thoughts into confusion.

"Lamia... Come closer..." they whispered again and again.

Her hands trembled, her body aching from the weight of their call, but she couldn't move. It was as if an invisible force held her in place, keeping her rooted to the spot. Her breath grew shallow, and a cold sweat began to form on her skin. Still, she could not tear herself away from the portraits, from those hollow-eyed children who now seemed to be watching her with an unsettling intensity.

Suddenly, without warning, the whispers stopped. The silence that followed was deafening, louder than the voices had ever been. The absence of sound was suffocating, pressing down on Lamia as if the very air around her had been drained away. She couldn't breathe, couldn't think, couldn't move. It was as if the entire world had paused, holding its breath, waiting for something to happen.

And then, in the farthest corner of the room, Lamia noticed it.

A mirror.

At first, it was just a vague shape, a dark shadow in the distance, but as her eyes fixed on it, she could see the details. It was tall and imposing, its edges framed with intricate carvings that seemed to twist and writhe like dark vines. The surface of the glass was impossibly black, absorbing the light around it, reflecting nothing. It was a void, a deep, empty space that threatened to swallow everything in its path. And yet, even as it repelled the light, Lamia couldn't tear her gaze away from it.

The mirror seemed to be calling her, drawing her in with an invisible force.

The whispers started again, but this time, they weren't in her ears. They were inside her head, filling her mind, urging her to move, to step closer. "Lamia…" they called. "Lamia, come to the mirror…"

Her feet moved without her consent, her body compelled to obey the pull of the mirror. Step by step, she walked toward it, each footfall echoing loudly in the emptiness of the hall. The paintings of the children seemed to shift, their hollow eyes following her every movement. The room felt colder with each step, the air thick with an unnatural chill that made her skin crawl.

When she finally reached the mirror, Lamia hesitated. She could feel the coldness of the glass even before her fingers touched it. It was like standing before an abyss, a doorway to something far more ancient and dangerous than she could ever understand. But the pull was too strong. She reached out, her fingers trembling as they brushed against the surface of the mirror. The moment she touched it, everything around her seemed to shift, as if the world itself had been turned upside down. The walls of the hall twisted and warped, the air became thick with a heavy, suffocating presence, and the portraits of the children began to change, their faces contorting into twisted, grotesque expressions.

Lamia gasped as she stepped back, but before she could react, the glass of the mirror rippled, like water disturbed by a stone. It was no longer reflecting her own face. No, the mirror was showing something else now, something far darker.

At first, it was a vague blur, a shadowy figure that seemed to be reaching out from the depths of the glass. But as Lamia's eyes adjusted, the figure became clearer. It was her. Or at least, it looked like her. The reflection in the mirror was almost the same—her same features, her same dark hair—but there was something horribly wrong. Her eyes were empty, hollow, like the children in the paintings. Her skin was pale, sickly, and her mouth twisted into a grotesque smile that was not her own.

Lamia's heart raced, her blood running cold. She stepped back, but the mirror seemed to pull her in, the reflection in the glass growing clearer and clearer. It was as if the mirror wanted her to see it, to confront whatever darkness lay within.

And then, suddenly, the whispering voices returned, louder than ever before. They filled her head, deafening and sharp, calling her name again and again. "Lamia... Lamia... come closer..."

She couldn't escape. The mirror was not just a reflection of her—it was a doorway, a portal into something darker, something she didn't fully understand. But it was clear now that the mirror had been waiting for her. It had been calling her, drawing her closer, pulling her into its depths. And as the voices grew louder, Lamia knew that whatever lay beyond the mirror was not something she could turn away from. It was waiting for her, and it was a part of her now.

The world around her blurred, the hall, the portraits, the mirror—they all began to dissolve, melting away into darkness. Lamia felt herself falling, falling into the cold, empty space beyond the glass, the voices growing louder still, as if the darkness was closing in around her.

And in that moment, Lamia realized that Hollow Manor, the mirror, the strange dreams—everything was connected. It wasn't just a dream. It wasn't just a nightmare. It was her past, her present, and her future, all wrapped up together in a tangled mess of shadows and whispers.

The mirror had been waiting for her to find the truth. And now, she was about to learn it—whether she was ready or not.

The House Awaits

The mansion had been standing for what felt like an eternity. Fifty long years had passed since the mysterious disappearance of its owner, Harold Hollow, and the many children who once lived there. The mansion had always been a topic of hushed conversations among the villagers, but no one really knew what had happened to them. And no one wanted to know. It was far easier to whisper about curses and ghosts, about haunting shadows and the darker things that lurked within the walls of the manor. Over the years, those whispered stories turned into legends, and those legends turned into warnings.

Lamia had always known of the mansion. It had been one of those stories she heard as a child, a tale designed to keep little ones from straying too far from home. "Stay close to the village," her mother had warned. "Don't go near Hollow Manor. It's a cursed place." But as she grew older, Lamia began to wonder whether the stories were just that—stories. She grew curious about the mansion, about the mystery that clung to it like cobwebs in the corners of a forgotten room.

Despite the warnings, she had never set foot inside Hollow Manor. She had heard about it all her life but had never dared venture close. Not until now. Now, something felt different. The pull to enter, to uncover the truth, was irresistible. It was as though the house itself had been calling her, beckoning her in with a soft whisper that she couldn't ignore.

The evening air was cool, and the sky was growing darker as she walked through the overgrown path that led to the mansion. The tall grass on either side of the path swayed in the breeze, and the trees above her creaked in the wind, their branches twisting like skeletal hands reaching toward the sky. The ground was uneven, the stones in the path cracked and worn from years of neglect. The mansion loomed ahead of her, its tall silhouette framed against the darkening sky. It was an imposing sight, with windows that seemed to stare back at her, empty and unblinking.

The iron gate creaked as she pushed it open. It was rusted and seemed to protest against the movement, but with a little effort, it gave way. Lamia stood for a moment at the entrance, her heart beating faster in her chest, her breath coming a little more quickly than usual. She wasn't sure what she expected to feel, but she knew she had to go inside. She had to understand why the mansion had been calling her, why she felt such a strange pull toward it.

As she stepped forward, the wind seemed to pick up around her, rushing past her ears like an invisible force. She shivered, but she wasn't sure if it was the cold or something else—something more sinister—that made her skin crawl. Her feet moved almost on their own, carrying her toward the mansion's grand entrance. The massive double doors stood before her, half open as if they were waiting for her to push them the rest of the way.

With a deep breath, she grabbed the handle and pushed. The door groaned as it moved, the wood creaking under the strain, and for a moment, Lamia thought it might collapse entirely. But it didn't. The door swung open slowly, revealing the dark hallway beyond. A cold draft swept past her, making her hair stand on end.

The house was quiet. Too quiet. It was a silence so complete it was almost deafening. The air inside was thick, filled with the smell of old wood and dust, the scent of something forgotten. As Lamia stepped over the threshold, she could feel the weight of the mansion pressing down on her, like the house was holding its breath, waiting for her next move. She looked around, her eyes adjusting to the dim light that filtered through the cracked windows.

The walls were lined with faded wallpaper, torn in places and peeling at the corners. The floorboards groaned under her weight as she moved deeper into the hallway, each step echoing in the silence. The furniture, once elegant and grand, was now covered in layers of dust. Some pieces had been overturned, as if someone had left in a hurry, while others lay abandoned in their original places. Everything in the house seemed frozen in time, left to decay slowly and quietly in the dark.

Her heart was pounding, but Lamia couldn't stop herself from exploring further. Something inside her urged her on, pushing her deeper into the mansion's dark corners, as if the house itself was guiding her. The longer she stood in the hallway, the more familiar the place felt. She couldn't explain it, but there was something about the house, something about the air itself, that made her feel as if she had been here before. As if she had lived here long ago.

The walls seemed to close in on her as she continued walking, her footsteps soft but steady on the worn floorboards. The silence was oppressive, and Lamia felt a growing sense of unease, as if she were being watched. She turned a corner and found herself in what seemed to be a large entryway. There was a grand staircase at the center, leading up to the second floor. The wood of the stairs was dark, and the railing was twisted, as if shaped by something ancient.

Lamia hesitated for a moment before she began to climb the stairs. They creaked under her weight, each step echoing in the stillness. The air grew colder the higher she went, and she could feel the hairs on the back of her neck standing up. The feeling of being watched grew stronger with every step she took. She could almost hear whispers in the shadows, soft and distant, as if the house was speaking to her in a language she couldn't quite understand.

At the top of the stairs, she found herself facing a long hallway. The doors on either side were closed, their surfaces scratched and worn. The walls were lined with more portraits, but these were different from the ones in the village. These portraits were of children, their faces pale and their eyes hollow, staring at her with an unsettling emptiness. The longer she looked at them, the more their eyes seemed to follow her, their gazes unblinking, unmoving.

One door at the far end of the hallway was slightly ajar, a thin sliver of darkness beyond it. Lamia felt an undeniable pull toward it, like something inside was calling to her, urging her to step closer.

With a mix of trepidation and curiosity, she made her way toward the door. As she pushed it open, a cold breeze rushed out from the room, carrying with it the scent of old wood and dust. Lamia stepped inside, her heart pounding as she looked around.

The room was bare, save for one thing—a large, ornate mirror standing against the far wall. It was unlike any mirror she had ever seen. The frame was dark and twisted, carved with strange symbols and faces, some of them half-finished, as if they had been left incomplete. The mirror itself was dark, almost black, and as Lamia stared into it, she could see her own reflection, but it was wrong.

At first, it was just a flicker, like a shadow moving in the glass. But as she looked closer, her reflection changed completely. The figure in the mirror was no longer her. Instead, it was a twisted version of herself—pale, hollow-eyed, and smiling in a way that made her blood run cold.

Lamia took a step back, her heart racing in her chest, but the figure in the mirror didn't move. It stayed there, grinning at her, its eyes empty and void of any warmth.

She couldn't tear her eyes away from it. The longer she stared, the more she felt herself drawn into the mirror, as though the figure on the other side were reaching out for her.

The room seemed to grow darker, the air thicker, and the whispers returned, soft at first but growing louder, surrounding her, filling her mind with a thousand voices all calling her name.

"Lamia..." they whispered, "come closer..."

The voice was low and familiar, as though it had been calling to her for years. A cold shiver ran down her spine as she realized that the house had been waiting for her. It had been calling her all along, and now, there was no turning back.

Echoes of the Children

At first, Lamia wasn't sure what was happening. She thought maybe it was just another strange dream. The walls around her seemed to move, like they were breathing, and her reflection showed up in every window she passed. Everywhere she turned, she saw herself staring back at her, but it wasn't like a normal reflection. It felt wrong somehow. Her heart pounded faster, and her breath caught in her throat as she tried to make sense of it all. This couldn't be real, could it?

But the more she looked, the more she knew. This wasn't a dream. Everything around her felt too real, too alive. The house, Hollow Manor, was alive in a way that made Lamia's skin crawl. It wasn't just the way the walls seemed to breathe or how the mirrors showed her reflection in strange ways. It was everything. The air felt heavy, thick, and cold. The silence was too much to bear, like it was pressing against her, suffocating her. She could feel the house watching her, listening to her every movement.

The further she went into the house, the more she felt the strange pull. It was like the house was calling to her, whispering things she couldn't quite understand. Every step she took felt like she was being drawn deeper into something she couldn't escape. The halls were long and dark, and the rooms were filled with old furniture covered in dust. But no matter how old and abandoned the place seemed, it still felt alive.

Lamia stepped cautiously into one of the rooms, her heart racing with every step. The room was large, and the only light came from the small windows high on the walls. She looked around, taking in the faded wallpaper and the old furniture that had been left behind. It felt like no one had been here in years. But something wasn't right. The room felt... different. It wasn't just an empty room; it felt like it had a memory, like it had been waiting for her.

Then she heard it.

At first, it was soft, like a faint whisper. It was almost too quiet to hear, but Lamia could just make out the sound of what seemed like children laughing. It was faint, but it was there, and it made the hairs on the back of her neck stand up. The laughter wasn't happy or carefree, though. It was sad, like it had been trapped here for a long time.

Lamia's eyes darted around the room, but there was no one there. She listened closely, straining to hear the laughter again. And then, just as she thought it was gone, it came back—louder this time. She could hear it coming from every direction, echoing through the walls of the house. The laughter was strange, twisted, and it made her feel cold inside.

She turned and hurried down the hallway, trying to shake the feeling of being watched. But the laughter followed her, echoing off the walls, growing louder with each step. The house seemed to be alive with it, as if it were part of the house itself.

Lamia's mind raced as she tried to understand what was happening. What was this laughter? And why did it sound so wrong? It was like the house itself was full of memories, memories of children who had been trapped here long ago, children who had disappeared and never been seen again. Their laughter filled the air, and it felt like it had been here for years, maybe even longer.

Lamia kept moving, drawn by the sound, her footsteps echoing in the quiet halls. The deeper she went, the more the laughter seemed to surround her. It wasn't just in her ears anymore. It was in her head, in her mind, whispering to her, calling to her. She felt like she was losing herself, like the house was pulling her into its dark, twisted heart.

She passed through another room, and this time, she froze. In the center of the room was an old table, and on the table sat a doll. It was a strange doll, not like any she had ever seen. It had wide, empty eyes and a pale face that seemed to stare at her. It wasn't a doll that looked like it had been played with recently. No, it looked like it had been here for a long time, just waiting.

Lamia took a step closer, unable to look away from the doll. It felt like the doll was looking back at her, its empty eyes staring right through her. The air around her seemed to grow colder as she stepped closer, her breath coming out in visible puffs.

Then, as if on its own, the doll's head turned slightly. Lamia's heart skipped a beat. She stumbled back, her breath catching in her throat. She had been sure the doll was still, but now it had moved. Her hand shook as she reached out toward it, unsure why she felt so drawn to it.

But as her fingers brushed against the cold porcelain of the doll, a strange feeling surged through her. It wasn't just cold—it was like touching something that shouldn't be touched, something that didn't belong in this world.

Suddenly, the whispers came back. Louder than before, more urgent, more frantic. "Lamia... come closer... don't be afraid..." The voices were everywhere now, swirling around her, filling her mind with their desperate cries.

Lamia stepped back, trying to pull away from the doll, but it felt like the house was holding her in place. The laughter of the children grew louder, the whispers becoming more intense, and she could feel the walls of the house closing in on her. It was as if the very air around her was alive with the voices of the children, their lost souls trapped in the house, unable to escape.

She could feel her heart racing, the fear rising in her chest. The house was pulling her in, and there was nothing she could do to stop it. She had to get out. She had to leave.

But just as she turned to run, she heard the sound of footsteps behind her. They were light, almost like the footsteps of a child. Lamia's heart skipped a beat. She turned quickly, but there was no one there. The house was empty, or so it seemed.

The laughter came again, louder this time, and the walls seemed to shake with it. Lamia turned and fled, her footsteps echoing through the halls. She didn't look back, not even once. She knew that something was following her, something that wanted to keep her here, trapped inside the walls of Hollow Manor forever.

The laughter of the children, the whispers, the darkness—they were all a part of the house now. And Lamia, whether she liked it or not, was part of it too.

A Portrait of Dread

Suddenly, Lamia stopped dead in her tracks. The room around her began to shift and blur, her heartbeat pounding in her ears. The walls of the grand hall stretched, growing taller, darker, as if the very mansion itself was breathing. She had been here before, in the dream, but now it felt so much more real—so much more dangerous.

The dust in the air hung thickly, catching the dim light that filtered through the cracks in the mansion's windows. Her breath came in shallow, quick bursts, her body frozen in place as she gazed at the large mirror standing in the center of the room. It was old, cracked in places, and covered in a layer of dust that seemed to belong to centuries of neglect. But despite its age, there was something about it—something about the way it seemed to pulse with energy—that made her feel like it was alive, waiting for her.

Around her, the walls were lined with portraits. At first, they looked like the typical paintings of children, their faces frozen in time, innocent smiles on their faces. But as Lamia stepped closer, she saw that their eyes were wrong. Their eyes were hollow, black voids that stared out from the canvas with an eerie emptiness. They seemed to watch her, their gaze following her every movement. A cold chill ran down her spine as she felt their eyes on her, unblinking, unfeeling.

She took a deep breath, trying to steady herself, and turned her attention back to the mirror. Her reflection stared back at her—exactly as she expected. But as she stepped closer to the mirror, her gaze fell upon one of the portraits hanging just beside it. Her heart skipped a beat as she realized what she was seeing.

There, in the middle of the row of portraits, was a painting of a young girl. Her face was pale, her eyes just as hollow as the others, but there was something about her that struck Lamia with a sense of dread. Something in the tilt of the girl's head, in the way she seemed to look directly at her, made Lamia's blood run cold.

It was her.

The girl in the portrait was her.

Lamia's breath caught in her throat. Her mind raced, trying to make sense of what she was seeing. This couldn't be right. How could it be her? How could a portrait of her be hanging in this place, in this room, with the other children who had vanished so many years ago? The confusion turned to panic as the walls around her seemed to close in, the air growing heavier with each passing second.

She turned from the mirror, her hands shaking as she reached out toward the portrait. Her fingers brushed the surface of the canvas, and for a moment, she thought she might fall through the painting, swallowed by the dark voids of the child's eyes. The room seemed to spin as she touched the frame, her fingers leaving trails of dust behind.

That was when the whispers began.

Soft at first, like the rustling of wind through dry leaves. But then they grew louder, more insistent. The voices of children, calling her name, crying for her, as if they had been waiting for her all this time. Their words tangled together, unintelligible at first, but then a single sentence emerged from the chaos, clear and chilling.

"Find us... before it's too late."

Lamia stumbled backward, her heart hammering in her chest. She could feel the presence of the children, their spirits trapped in the walls of the house, their voices echoing in her mind. It was as if they were all around her, closing in from every direction. She wanted to scream, to run, but she couldn't move. She was rooted to the spot, her eyes locked on the portrait—the one of her.

The whispers continued, filling the room with an overwhelming sense of urgency. "You belong here... You always have." The voices were now mingling with the laughter, the same twisted sound she had heard before, filling the air with an unbearable heaviness.

Lamia tried to tear her eyes away from the portrait, but it was impossible. She couldn't look away. The face of the girl in the painting seemed to change, shifting slightly, the hollow eyes becoming deeper, darker, as if they were pulling her in. Her reflection in the mirror blurred, distorting until it no longer looked like her own. The reflection twisted, as if mocking her, laughing in her face.

Suddenly, the room grew cold, and Lamia could see her breath in front of her, misting in the air. The portraits around her seemed to move, their eyes flicking to new positions, following her every movement. The laughter grew louder, and the whispering became frantic, urging her to understand, to accept her place in the house.

Her legs shook, but she forced herself to look away from the portrait and turn toward the door. She needed to get out. She needed to leave before she was trapped here forever. But as she tried to move, the room shifted again. The walls closed in on her, the door now impossibly far away. The whispers grew louder, drowning out everything else, until Lamia felt like she was suffocating.

"Lamia…" The voice was clear now, a single voice cutting through the rest, a voice she recognized—her own. The voice of the girl in the portrait, speaking directly to her. "Come closer. You belong with us."

The room seemed to twist, bending around her as the walls stretched toward her, trying to pull her back in. Lamia felt herself being dragged toward the mirror, toward the portrait, unable to stop herself. Her heart raced, and she tried to scream, but her voice was lost in the sound of the children's laughter, the echo of their whispers.

"No!" she cried out, desperate to escape. But the more she struggled, the more the house seemed to push back. The air grew colder, and she could feel the weight of the mansion's past pressing down on her, threatening to consume her.

She had to find a way out. She had to escape the curse that had bound her to this place. But before she could move, the whispering stopped. The laughter ceased. The room fell silent, and for a brief moment, Lamia thought she had won. She dared to hope, to believe that she could break free.

But then, as if in response to her thoughts, the walls seemed to collapse inward, and the floor beneath her feet cracked open. The mansion groaned, its bones creaking as if it were alive, and the room seemed to spin uncontrollably. Lamia reached out, her hands desperately searching for anything to hold onto, but there was nothing.

And then, just as quickly as it had all begun, everything went dark.

Lamia's body went limp, her mind swirling in a haze of confusion. Was she dreaming again? Had she really been there? Was the mansion even real? The answers eluded her as the darkness closed in.

But as the darkness consumed her, she felt a strange warmth. A soft whisper tickled her ear, the voice clearer now than ever before.

“You’re not alone,” it said. “You never were.”

And in that moment, Lamia knew the truth.

She wasn’t just a visitor in Hollow Manor. She was a part
of it.

The Fall into Darkness

Lamia stood frozen, her eyes locked on the portrait of the child with hollow, dark eyes. Her reflection stared back at her with a cold emptiness that made her blood run cold. How could this be? How could she, a girl who had never been to Hollow Manor before, be staring back from a painting that had no right to exist? The walls around her seemed to close in, and her heart began to race as she felt a growing sense of dread. This couldn't be happening.

She had heard the stories, of course, the rumors that whispered in the village about the children who had gone missing. But she had always thought they were just that—stories. Folklore. A tale told to scare the young ones into behaving. But standing here now, in this mansion, with the dark eyes of a child staring back at her, she realized just how wrong she had been.

The silence of the room pressed in on her. The air felt thick, heavy with something she couldn't quite explain. She tried to take a step back, but her feet felt as if they were stuck to the floor, unwilling to move. The whispers, those soft, eerie voices, filled the air again, like an old song that she couldn't remember the words to. They seemed to come from everywhere and nowhere, swirling around her and echoing in her ears. The voices of the children. She could hear them laughing, soft and sweet, their voices like music at first, but then fading into something darker, more sinister.

She couldn't escape them. The more she listened, the more they seemed to call her name. Lamia. Lamia. The sound of it, her name being pulled through the air, felt like a cold hand wrapping around her heart. It felt so familiar and yet so wrong. Was this the house calling to her? Was this the mansion that had been the cause of so much misery, of so many lost lives?

Her head spun as memories began to flood her mind, memories that were not hers, but somehow felt like they belonged to her. The more she tried to push them away, the more they came. She remembered being small, so small, and hearing the whispers in the wind, so soft and inviting. They had called to her then, just as they were calling to her now, drawing her toward this place, this house that had been abandoned for so long.

It was as though the house itself had a mind of its own, a mind that had been watching her, waiting for her. The moment she had stepped into this place, she had sealed her fate. There was no going back now. Lamia could feel it deep in her bones, the weight of the house's grip tightening around her. The painting of the child, her hollow-eyed twin, seemed to mock her, its eyes following her every movement. How could this be? How could it know her? Why was her image in this place?

The more she stared at the painting, the more she saw. Her reflection—her face—was no longer just a reflection. It began to twist, to change, as if it were alive. The hollow eyes in the portrait began to blink, the lips stretching into a smile that was not hers. It was like the painting was breathing, moving in a way that no painting should. And then, in the stillness of the room, something else happened.

The air grew colder, biting and sharp, as if the very temperature of the room had dropped to an impossible degree. Lamia shivered, her breath coming out in little puffs of white, her body trembling with fear. She wanted to scream, to run, but the whispers—the voices—were too loud now. They surrounded her, grew louder and louder, until the sound of them was deafening. They were coming from the walls, from the floor, from the ceiling. They were everywhere.

And then, everything went silent. The quiet was so sudden, so absolute, that it felt like the entire house had stopped breathing. Lamia's heart pounded in her chest, her body frozen in place. The whispers were gone, but now there was something else—something far worse. In the silence, she could hear the sound of footsteps, slow and deliberate, coming closer, closer to her.

Lamia didn't know where the footsteps were coming from. She didn't know how they could exist when there was no one else in the house. But she could hear them, feel them, as though they were walking directly behind her. She turned quickly, but there was no one there. Only the dark, empty rooms of the mansion.

Her eyes fell back to the portrait. It was different now. The child in the painting—her, the girl with hollow eyes—was no longer just a reflection. The eyes seemed to follow her every move, no longer empty, but filled with something dark and knowing. They were looking at her, and for the first time, she realized the truth. It wasn't just the house that had been waiting for her. It had been her all along.

She had been drawn to the house as a child. She had wandered too close, just as the others had. She had been a part of this all along, connected to this place in a way that she couldn't understand. The house had claimed her once before, when she was young, and now, it was calling her back.

The footsteps grew louder. She spun around again, but there was no one there. Nothing. Only the darkness. And yet, she could feel them—feel the presence of something standing behind her, something watching her with cold, unblinking eyes.

It was then that Lamia realized that she was no longer just a visitor. She wasn't just a girl who had wandered into Hollow Manor. She had always been part of it, always connected to it in ways that she hadn't understood before. The mansion had claimed her once. And now, it was calling her back, pulling her deeper into its depths, into the darkness.

Lamia took a deep breath, her chest tightening, her mind spinning. She didn't know if she could escape. She didn't know if anyone ever had. The footsteps were closer now, closer than ever. She felt the presence behind her grow stronger, felt the weight of it pressing down on her shoulders.

And then, just as quickly as the footsteps had started, they stopped.

The air grew even colder, the silence now overwhelming. Lamia was paralyzed with fear, her heart racing in her chest. She knew, without a doubt, that she was not alone.

And she never would be again.

Harold Hollow's Truth

Everything Lamia had ever known—everything she thought she understood—was a lie. Her memories, her life in the village, her kind aunt who had raised her, even the small, comforting mirror that hung on her wall—none of it was true. It was all part of a false world, a carefully woven illusion. The key to everything had always been there, right in front of her, and yet she had never fully understood it. That key was the mirror. The mirror wasn't just a reflection. It wasn't just glass. It was something much more. It was a doorway, a bridge between two worlds, and the world she had been living in was just a shadow.

As the realization struck her, she felt the floor tremble beneath her feet. Her heart skipped a beat, and for a moment, she thought she was imagining it. But then, the ground beneath her cracked open with a loud, terrifying sound. Before she could even react, she felt herself fall, the darkness swallowing her whole as she plunged into the unknown.

She landed hard on the cold, rough floor of a dark, musty cellar. The air was thick with dust and decay, the smell of rot in the air. She gasped, her lungs burning as she tried to catch her breath. The fall had knocked the wind out of her, and for a moment, all she could do was lay there, staring up into the inky blackness above her. She could barely make out the faint outline of the room, the walls so dark and thick with shadows that it felt as though they were closing in around her.

Slowly, Lamia pushed herself up. Her body ached from the fall, but the pain was nothing compared to the feeling of dread crawling up her spine. Something was wrong here. Something was terribly wrong. Her instincts screamed at her to run, but there was nowhere to go. The cellar felt like a trap, a cage, and she could feel the weight of the darkness pressing in from all sides.

As her eyes adjusted to the dim light, she saw a figure in the center of the room. At first, it was just a vague shape, hard to make out in the shadows. But then, the figure stepped forward, and Lamia froze. She could feel the blood drain from her face, and her heart thudded in her chest. There, standing before her, was Harold Hollow.

He was tall and thin, his skin a pale, sickly gray. His face was gaunt, drawn, as though he hadn't eaten in years. His eyes, however, were the most unsettling part. They were empty. Hollow. There were no pupils, no light. Just dark, endless voids where eyes should have been. It was like looking into the abyss of nothingness, and Lamia felt her stomach twist in horror.

He gazed at her for a long moment, his expression unreadable. The silence stretched out between them, thick and suffocating, until he spoke.

"You've finally come back," Harold Hollow rasped, his voice low and rough, as if he hadn't used it in years. "But you never really left, did you?"

Lamia's breath caught in her throat. She didn't know what to say. She didn't know how to respond to this man who had been a ghost in her life for so long. Who was he? What was he talking about? She had never seen him before. She had never been to this place. She had never been part of whatever nightmare this was. But the way he said it, the way his hollow eyes bored into hers, made her feel like she had always known him. Like he was something familiar—something she couldn't quite place, but something that had always been there, lurking in the background.

"What do you mean?" Lamia whispered, her voice shaking. "Who are you?"

Harold Hollow took a slow step forward, his movements deliberate, as though savoring the moment. He tilted his head slightly, studying her. His lips curled into a small, almost imperceptible smile.

"Who am I?" he repeated, his voice softer now, as if amused by her confusion. "I am the one who has been waiting for you. All this time. I've always been waiting. You've always known me, even when you didn't remember."

Lamia's mind spun. She stepped back, her body trembling with fear. She wanted to turn and run, but she was frozen in place, caught by the weight of his words. What was he saying? How could she have known him if she had never met him before? She had never heard of him before, not in this way. He was just a name in the stories—the man who had vanished with the children, the man who had left Hollow Manor a cursed place. She had never believed the stories. They were just that—stories. But now, standing here in front of him, she felt something deep inside her telling her that those stories weren't just made up. They were real. And this man—this thing standing in front of her—was part of it.

"Your memories," Harold Hollow said, his voice growing more distant and cold, "they're not yours. The life you think you've lived, the family you think you've had—they're all a lie. You were never meant to be part of their world. You were meant to be here. With me."

Lamia's stomach twisted into knots. Her life was a lie? Her aunt, her village, her home—everything she had known, everything she had believed in, was false? She felt as though the ground was slipping from under her. She had thought she was just a normal girl, living a normal life. But now, standing here in this dark, horrible place, she understood that it was never that simple. There was a truth that had been hidden from her, a truth she couldn't fully grasp, but now she was beginning to see it.

"You've always been mine," Harold Hollow continued, his voice smooth and eerie, as though this was the most natural thing in the world. "And now, you will stay with me. Forever."

Lamia's blood ran cold. The room felt smaller now, the air heavier, as though the walls themselves were closing in. The cellar seemed to darken, the shadows stretching out like fingers reaching for her. She could feel it—the weight of his words, the weight of this place, pressing down on her. She wanted to scream. She wanted to fight. But deep down, she knew there was no escape. There was no way out.

This was her reality. Hollow Manor was her true home. The mirror had been the key to her past, and now that past had caught up with her. There was no turning back. She had been part of this twisted story all along.

And now, there was nowhere to run.

The House's Hunger

Lamia's heart hammered in her chest, her breath shallow and panicked. She opened her mouth to speak, but no words came out. It felt as though the very air around her was thickening, pressing in on her from all sides, stifling her. Every part of her wanted to run, to escape this horrible, twisted place, but her legs felt like lead. The dread that washed over her was suffocating, and she could barely move, let alone think clearly.

Harold Hollow's voice sliced through the silence, cold and unnervingly calm. "Hollow Manor," he said, his voice dripping with something dark, something ancient, "is not just haunted. It is alive. It has always been alive."

Lamia's pulse quickened. What did he mean by that? The words didn't make sense, and yet, deep inside, she knew that he wasn't lying. The weight of the house, the way it seemed to watch her, the feeling of being trapped, it was all real. The walls, the floors, the rooms—they weren't just stone and wood. They had a pulse, a rhythm, as though the manor itself had a heart that beat in time with hers. It was almost as if it were waiting for something. Waiting for her.

"Do you know what this place is?" Harold asked, his hollow eyes boring into her. "Do you understand why it calls to you? It is more than just a house. It is a prison. A prison for souls. And you, Lamia, are one of them."

Her mind spun in confusion. She couldn't breathe, couldn't think. She didn't understand. She was just a girl, just someone who had stumbled into this nightmare. She had never been part of anything like this. She was just… normal. She had been living her life. She had been… alive. But now, as Harold's words settled in, she felt something deep inside her begin to unravel. It was like a dark curtain being drawn back, revealing a truth she had never known—could never have known.

"The children who have gone missing," Harold continued, his voice lower now, tinged with something far more sinister, "they are not gone. They are here, in this house, trapped. Their souls are bound to the manor, forced to live out endless cycles of false lives. Do you hear their whispers? Can you feel their presence? They are part of this place. Just like you will be, once you understand. Once you accept."

Lamia's eyes widened. The missing children—the ones the village had whispered about for years—had never truly disappeared. They hadn't been taken by some terrible fate. They had become part of the house. Part of the twisted existence that Hollow Manor had claimed. Their spirits were locked in the walls, living over and over again in a loop that they could never escape.

She felt sick, her stomach lurching. The idea that she was no different than them, that she might soon join them in their endless torment, filled her with horror. She had always believed in simple things—her life had been so normal, so ordinary. But now, everything she had ever known felt like a lie. This place, this house, was something beyond her understanding. And yet, it was tied to her in ways she couldn't escape.

"Why?" Lamia finally managed to croak, her voice weak, trembling. "Why me? Why am I here? I'm not like them. I'm not one of them."

Harold's laugh was soft, eerie. "You think you're different? You think you can escape?" His eyes darkened. "This house chooses who it wants. It sees the broken pieces of your soul. It knows you better than you know yourself. You have always been part of this place, Lamia. Always."

Lamia staggered backward, her mind racing. She tried to make sense of the chaos in her head, the confusion that clouded her thoughts. She had thought she was just a normal girl, just a daughter of her aunt, living in a village. She had never asked for this. She had never wanted this. But somehow, it seemed like Hollow Manor had always known her. It had always been waiting for her.

"The mirror," she whispered, her eyes wide as the pieces began to fall into place. "The mirror in my room. It... it led me here. It's the key, isn't it? The key to the manor, the key to everything."

Harold's smile deepened. "Yes. The mirror has always been the link between the real world and this place. It shows you what you want to see. It pulls you in, leads you here, where you belong. It is the manor's way of calling to you.

It's not just glass. It's a doorway—a doorway that will lead you back. Back to the house."

Lamia felt the walls around her seem to close in, the weight of the truth settling heavily on her chest. It was too much to take in, too much to understand. She didn't want to believe it. She didn't want to accept that her life—her normal, happy life—had never been real. But the more she thought about it, the more she realized that Harold was right. There was no escape. The house had already claimed her. It had been waiting for her to realize it. The missing children were a part of it, and so was she.

"Why do you want me here?" Lamia asked, her voice shaking with fear. "What do you want from me?"

Harold stepped closer, his hollow eyes never leaving her face. "I don't want anything from you, Lamia. The manor does. It wants your soul. It wants your life. And it will have it. Eventually."

The air in the cellar seemed to grow heavier, colder, as Lamia's heart pounded in her chest. She wanted to scream, to run, to get out of this place. But the house, the walls, the very ground beneath her feet seemed to hold her in place. She was trapped, caught in a nightmare that she could never wake up from.

The truth was clear now. Hollow Manor was alive. It was waiting for her. And there was nowhere left to run.

It had already begun.

The Cycle of Horror

Lamia stood frozen, the weight of the truth crashing down on her like a heavy stone. She had always wondered why she felt so drawn to Hollow Manor, why the mirror called to her with such a relentless, almost desperate longing. Now, she knew. It wasn't just curiosity that had brought her here—it was fate.

The dark, air of the cellar seemed to close in around her, thick and suffocating, as if the house itself were watching, waiting for her to fully understand what had happened. Her gaze drifted to the corners of the room, to the shadows that seemed to shift and sway on their own. It was as if the very walls were breathing, alive with the souls that had been trapped there for so long.

She had been one of them. One of the children who had disappeared all those years ago. But somehow, she hadn't died like the others. Instead, the house had taken her in a different way—like a parasite, it had taken a part of her soul and twisted it, molding her into its servant. She was no longer fully alive, not fully dead either. She existed in a state of perpetual limbo, neither a full soul nor a lost one.

Her reflection in the mirror—the hollow-eyed version of herself—wasn't just a reflection at all. It was the part of her that the house had claimed. The part of her that never slept, that always watched, that waited for the moment when she would return. The moment when the cycle would start again.

Lamia had been a child when she first entered the house, drawn in by the whispers and the promise of secrets hidden within its dark, decaying walls. She had wandered in, just like all the others, and like all the others, she had been trapped. But while the others had lost their lives, she had lost something far worse. Her freedom. Her soul.

Every time she tried to escape, the house would pull her back. The mirror would call to her, and she would find herself drawn to it, unable to resist its pull. It had become a cruel game—her life was a series of false starts, moments of hope and freedom followed by a sudden, brutal return to the house. Each time she tried to leave, the house would remind her of its power.

Her hollow-eyed reflection was the manifestation of that power. It was the piece of her that the house controlled, the part of her that could never escape. Every time she looked into the mirror, it was there, watching her, silently reminding her of the truth: she was its prisoner.

The children who had vanished before her—they were still here, too. Trapped in the walls of the manor, their souls bound to it for eternity. They existed in a kind of suspended animation, living out endless cycles of fake lives. Some of them were trapped in the past, others in the future. Some were stuck in memories they couldn't escape. But none of them were truly free.

Lamia's mind swirled with confusion and terror. How long had she been trapped in this cycle? How many years had passed since she first entered the house? She couldn't remember. Time had no meaning here. Days bled into nights, and moments stretched on forever, until she wasn't sure whether she was still alive or just another ghost in the house, a prisoner of its insatiable hunger.

As she looked around the cellar, she saw the faces of the other children. They were there, standing in the shadows, their hollow eyes staring at her with the same mixture of fear and resignation that she felt. They had been here for so long, lost in the endless cycles of the manor, that they had almost forgotten what it was like to be free. Almost.

The air in the room grew colder, and Lamia felt a chill run down her spine. She knew what she had to do. The house had to be stopped, and she was the only one who could do it. But how? She had tried before, only to be dragged back every time.

The mirror. The house's connection to the outside world was through the mirror, she realized. It was the key to breaking the cycle. If she could destroy it, if she could somehow sever the link between the house and the mirror, she might be able to free herself and the others.

But the mirror was powerful. She had felt its pull every time she tried to leave, every time she had hoped to escape. The house was built around it, and destroying it wouldn't be easy.

Lamia looked at the other children, their hollow eyes watching her. She could feel their pain, their longing for freedom. They had all been trapped here, but maybe—just maybe—they could help her. Maybe together, they could break the cycle.

But first, Lamia had to find a way to confront the mirror once and for all.

The cycle of horror had been set into motion long ago, but it was up to her to end it. And this time, she wouldn't let the house win.

The Awakening

Lamia's mind reeled as Harold's words sank in, each revelation cutting deeper than the last. She wasn't just another soul trapped by the house—she was part of it, woven into its very essence. The truth was more horrible than anything she could have imagined. Hollow Manor had not only stolen her life; it had created her, shaped her into something dark and ancient, a creature of myth, designed to lure others into its endless grasp.

As she stood there, Harold's gaunt, shadowy figure watching her with that hollow stare, fragments of her forgotten past began to piece themselves together. It was as though she were waking from a deep sleep, memories resurfacing like broken shards of glass. She could see herself, not as she was now, but as she had been over and over again—different ages, different forms, always appearing before unsuspecting children as a friendly face, a trusted voice. She would speak to them softly, inviting them into the house's darkened halls, unaware of the terrible role she played.

A horrible chill washed over her as she remembered a young boy, barely six years old, his face round and innocent, his eyes wide with trust. She had led him through the manor's gates, down the creaking hallways, and into the darkness of the cellar. She could see him now, his frightened face looking up at her, his small hand clinging to hers. Her heart twisted painfully, and she wanted to reach out, to pull him back, to scream at her past self to stop—but the memory continued, mercilessly, and she watched as the boy faded into the shadows, his soul devoured by the manor.

The memories kept coming. A girl with a laugh like bells, a boy with a toy boat, a little girl clutching a stuffed bear—they had all followed her, believing her to be a friend, a guide, only to disappear into the manor's depths, lost forever. They had trusted her, and she had betrayed them, time and time again.

Harold's cold voice interrupted her thoughts. "You're not like the others," he whispered, his voice echoing through the dim room. "You were born from this place. You are its voice, its pull, its lure. Without you, the manor's hunger could never be satisfied."

Lamia's heart pounded as she struggled to breathe, her hands trembling as she realized the full weight of his words. She was more than just a victim of Hollow Manor; she was a part of it, a piece of its dark will, created to draw others into its grasp. Every time she had felt the pull to return, it was because the house needed her. The mirror had called her, reminding her of her purpose, forcing her back when she tried to leave.

She fell to her knees, the cold floor pressing against her skin, her mind racing with the horror of what she truly was. The reflection she had seen in the mirror—the hollow-eyed version of herself—wasn't just a reflection; it was her true self, the dark, empty creature the house had made her into. She hadn't just been haunted by the house;

she had been its servant, its willing accomplice, even when she didn't know it.

"I was... I was the one..." she choked, her voice barely a whisper, filled with disbelief and self-loathing. "I led them all here. I was the reason they never left."

"Yes," Harold said, a cruel satisfaction glinting in his hollow gaze. "You were never meant to escape, Lamia. You were never meant to be free. You are part of this house, and you always will be."

A strange, quiet calm settled over her as his words sank in. If she was part of the manor, if she had been its servant all along, then perhaps she had the power to break free. The house had bound her, but maybe, just maybe, she could turn that power against it.

A faint flicker of determination sparked in her heart, a defiant flame that the house could not smother. She was tired of being a pawn, tired of being used. She would no longer be the creature that led innocent souls to their doom. She would fight, even if it meant turning against the very thing that had created her.

She looked up, meeting Harold's hollow eyes with a newfound resolve. "If I am part of this house," she said, her voice steady, "then I have the power to stop it. I don't have to be its servant. I can break free. I can set them all free."

Harold's expression twisted, and for the first time, she saw a flicker of fear in his eyes. He stepped back, as though her defiance had physically struck him. But his lips curled into a cruel smile. "You cannot escape your fate, Lamia. The house will not let you go."

Lamia stood, her fists clenched, her heart pounding with a fierce, wild hope. She didn't know how she would do it, but she knew one thing: she would fight. She would find a way to break the house's hold over her, to free the souls it had trapped, and to put an end to its twisted cycle of horror.

As she walked through the dark halls of the manor, the shadows seemed to grow thicker, as though the house itself sensed her defiance and was closing in on her, determined to crush her spirit. But Lamia held her head high, her steps unwavering. She was no longer the house's servant; she was its enemy, and she would not rest until it was destroyed.

The manor whispered around her, angry and restless, but Lamia pressed on, unafraid. She would find a way to break the cycle, to free herself and the souls of the children who had been lost. She would reclaim her soul, and she would not stop until the house's power was shattered once and for all.

Shadows in the Light

Lamia's heart thundered in her chest as she stood frozen, trapped in the dark, cold cellar. She'd just learned the truth—that every memory she held, every feeling she thought was hers, was nothing more than a trick spun by Hollow Manor. The house had made her, shaped her to its will, casting her in a role she had unknowingly played. She wasn't real, not in the way she had believed. She was a piece of the house—a living, breathing part of its dark purpose.

The walls around her seemed to close in, their ancient, rotting wood groaning as if in satisfaction. Shadows stretched along the floor like claws, eager to reach her. They were alive, she could feel it—a silent, whispering threat. They knew she understood now. And they weren't about to let her escape.

In the damp, icy air, she could almost hear the house breathe, its pulse slow and steady, like a creature stirring from a deep sleep. Each breath pulled her closer, and she felt its power, thick and heavy, pressing down on her, urging her to surrender, to accept her fate as its eternal prisoner. A sliver of terror ran down her spine. She realized she'd been led here, step by careful step, into the house's heart, where it was strongest. She was alone in its twisted grip.

With each passing second, her courage faded, and coldness seeped into her bones. The flickering shadows seemed to leer at her, mocking her discovery. The house had shown her those false lives, those pieces of joy and love, only to tighten its control. She saw it clearly now—the house didn't just want her body; it wanted her mind, her soul, every last piece of her.

As her fear thickened, the shadows pressed in close, their edges sharp and jagged, whispering her name in twisted, mocking tones. Her heartbeat quickened as she tried to turn away from the house's grip, but it felt like her feet were rooted to the ground, sinking into the very foundation of the cellar.

Then, a cold, slithering voice filled the room, echoing off the stone walls. "You are mine, Lamia," it hissed, scraping through her ears like a rusted blade. It was the house itself, speaking to her. Its voice was dark and empty, like something that had known nothing but death. "There is no escaping. You belong to me."

The walls seemed to pulse with a sickly, dark energy, closing tighter around her. The flickering lights overhead dimmed until they barely held a glow, casting her into near darkness. The portraits of children, once her companions in fear, were fading into the shadows. She felt her vision blur, her body weakening as though it, too, was becoming a shadow, slipping out of the world.

In her horror, she caught sight of her own reflection in the room's broken mirror, a hollow-eyed version of herself, pale and empty. The reflection's lips twisted into a sinister smile, watching her with cold, soulless eyes. She saw herself—her other self—smiling, as if reveling in her horror.

The voice continued, filling her mind. "You were made to lure them in, Lamia, to bring the children to me. They belong to the house, just as you do." She heard the echo of soft footsteps, felt the icy breath of those she had brought to this place. She could feel their sadness, their despair, lingering in the air like a thick fog, trapped and desperate, calling to her.

As her vision darkened, Lamia fought the feeling pulling her under. She felt the weight of the house's will pushing her down, forcing her to give in, to surrender. Her knees buckled as she struggled to stay upright, her breath ragged as if the very air had turned to dust.

The house's walls pulsed, beating with a slow, dark rhythm, like a twisted heart. The shadows clung to her skin, tightening around her wrists, her neck, pulling her down as if dragging her into the floor itself. Her body felt heavier, and she knew that if she didn't escape now, she never would.

In a last, desperate surge of strength, Lamia looked up, her voice barely a whisper but filled with every ounce of defiance left in her. "You don't own me," she spat, even as her voice cracked. She fought to keep the shadows from consuming her, fighting against the grip of the house, forcing herself to take one trembling step back, and then another.

But as she turned toward the doorway, the shadows reached out like fingers, tightening their grasp. She felt them dragging her back, pulling her closer to the walls, their dark voices rising to a feverish, hungry chorus, laughing at her helplessness.

"Run all you want, Lamia," the house whispered, its voice slithering through her mind. "But you will always belong to me."

As she staggered out of the cellar, the shadows clawed at her heels, filling her ears with dark, echoing laughter. Her heart raced as she stumbled up the stairs, the whispers chasing her, the darkness almost alive, breathing and reaching. With each step, she felt the house's grip loosen, but just barely, as if it were letting her go only to watch her come back, knowing it would call her again.

When she finally burst into the night air, the house's dark energy slipped back into the shadows, waiting, watching. As Lamia stumbled away, her mind spun with fear and defiance. She'd left the house for now, but she knew it wouldn't rest—it would call to her, whispering her name in the dead of night, waiting for her to return.

And deep down, she feared that one day, she would answer.

The Illusion of Freedom

Just as the darkness consumed her, Lamia awoke with a violent jolt, gasping for air. Her eyes flew open to blinding white lights above her. The harsh brightness stung her pupils, and she squinted, trying to make sense of her surroundings. She was in a hospital bed, a sterile white room enveloping her. The beeping of machines was the first sound she recognized, their rhythmic pulse steady and persistent. The scent of antiseptic and bleach hung heavy in the air.

Doctors and nurses bustled around her, moving with quick, practiced steps, checking machines, adjusting tubes, and murmuring to one another in hushed tones. One of the nurses, a woman with kind, soft eyes, looked down at her with a smile. "You've been in a coma for months," she said gently, her voice soothing but foreign to Lamia's ears.

A coma?

The word echoed in Lamia's mind, but it didn't make sense. What had happened? Where was she? How did she get here? Her heart thudded in her chest, but a strange emptiness lingered inside her, as if a part of her had been ripped away and she didn't know what it was.

"Where am I?" Lamia croaked, her voice hoarse, as though she hadn't used it in ages.

"You're in the hospital," the nurse replied, checking her vitals. "You've been unconscious for a long time. We were really worried about you."

But Lamia wasn't worried. She was confused. Her mind raced as she searched for answers. The house. The children. Harold Hollow. Was it all just a dream? A nightmare? She blinked rapidly, trying to clear the fog in her head, but the images—those haunting memories—kept rushing back.

The tall, crumbling walls of Hollow Manor. The whispers of the lost children. Harold Hollow, his empty eyes staring into her soul.

Lamia's breathing quickened as panic began to claw at her chest. It couldn't be real. None of it could be real. She was in a hospital, safe, wasn't she?

But then, she noticed something strange. A soft creaking sound came from the corner of the room, and she turned her head, her heart skipping a beat. There, in the far corner, was a figure standing in the shadows. It was hard to make out in the dim light, but Lamia felt its presence—strong, suffocating. Her chest tightened.

Her reflection.

She knew it before she even saw it. She didn't have to see the face to know what it was. She had seen that hollow-eyed figure too many times. It was always there, always waiting for her. The thing she had once thought was a figment of her imagination. But now, in the quiet of the hospital room, it was real.

Her reflection was there, and it was staring right at her.

A cold sweat broke out over Lamia's body. Her heart hammered in her chest as she tried to sit up, but her body felt heavy, sluggish. The machines beeped faster, the noise growing frantic, like the pulse of her own panic.

The reflection in the corner of the room didn't move, but its hollow eyes never left her. Slowly, the air grew thicker, colder, until it felt like she was suffocating.

Lamia's vision blurred, her thoughts became a jumbled mess. She couldn't think straight. She felt dizzy, light-headed, like she was being pulled under, pulled back into the darkness. Was it the coma? Was it a lingering effect of whatever had happened to her? Or was it the house—the house that had never really let her go?

"Get away from me," Lamia whispered, the words shaky. She wasn't sure if she was speaking to the reflection or to herself.

The shadow in the corner flickered. For a moment, Lamia thought she saw it move, but then it was gone. She blinked again, and when her eyes refocused, she was staring at a normal hospital room. The nurses and doctors were still bustling about, the machines still beeping in their usual, mechanical rhythm.

Lamia shook her head, trying to clear the confusion.

She turned to look at the mirror again. But this time, it was empty. No hollow-eyed reflection. No twisted figure staring at her.

Maybe it had all been in her head, she thought. Maybe it was a side effect of the coma.

But just as she was about to convince herself that it had all been a dream, the reflection reappeared, but this time, it wasn't just in the mirror. No, it was standing right in front of her—closer now, its hollow eyes glowing, staring straight into her soul. Lamia felt a cold shiver crawl down her spine.

The smile that curled on its lips was familiar, twisted, and empty.

"No, no, no…" Lamia breathed, her voice trembling. "This can't be real."

The reflection spoke, its voice low and echoing, as if it came from deep within the walls. "You can never escape, Lamia. You were always meant to be here. Always part of the house. The house never forgets its children."

Lamia tried to look away, tried to push herself back into the bed, but her body wouldn't move. She felt paralyzed, as if the very air around her was suffocating her, keeping her trapped. The reflection's grin grew wider, until it seemed to stretch too far, far beyond what a normal human face could do.

Suddenly, she felt herself falling. The ground beneath her seemed to disappear. The hospital room dissolved like smoke in the wind, replaced by a vast, dark emptiness.

Her heart raced as she fell deeper and deeper into the void.

The whispers returned.

Lamia... Lamia... Come closer... Come with us...

The sound of the children's voices grew louder, swirling around her, drowning out all other noise. She tried to scream, but no sound came from her mouth. She was falling—falling into the blackness.

When she landed, it wasn't with a thud, but with a soft, wet thump. Her body slumped forward, and she slowly lifted her head, blinking against the dark, oppressive fog that surrounded her.

She was in a different place now, a place that felt wrong, suffocating. The walls were lined with mirrors, cracked and covered with dust. The air smelled of mildew, of old rot, of decay. The very ground beneath her feet seemed unstable, like it could crumble away at any moment.

She wasn't alone.

There, standing in front of her, was the figure—the one with hollow eyes, the one that had always been there, always following her. It stood tall, its face twisted into a grin that was both terrifying and unnatural.

"You're finally home," it said, its voice like a distant echo in her mind, speaking from a place she couldn't see.

Lamia's heart pounded in her chest as she realized the truth. She had never escaped the house. The house had never let her go.

"You belong here," the figure said, its voice almost sweet now, coaxing her, drawing her in. "You always have."

Lamia's legs felt weak beneath her. She couldn't escape. She couldn't run. The house had her, and it was never going to let her go.

The mirrors around her began to ripple, the surfaces distorting, showing twisted, distorted images of the children—some smiling, some crying, some reaching out for her, their faces full of despair.

And Lamia knew, deep within her, that there was no escape.

She was never going to wake up.

The mirrors cracked, and the darkness swallowed her whole.

The True Nature of Lamia

As the days passed, Lamia's world felt like it was shifting underneath her, just out of reach, as if the very ground she stood on was unstable. She tried to push the feelings away, but they wouldn't leave. Every time she looked into the mirror, her reflection seemed... off. At first, it was small things—a blink that didn't match, a movement that felt just a second too slow. But soon, the differences became more obvious. Her reflection would stare at her with hollow eyes, grinning when she wasn't. Sometimes, it would even make gestures she hadn't intended, like mimicking her movements, but twisting them into something wrong, something... menacing.

At night, the shadows in her room grew longer, stretching out from the corners, curling around the edges of the furniture like fingers reaching for her. Lamia would turn to look, but by the time her eyes focused, they were gone. It was as though they only existed in the corner of her vision, always waiting, always moving when she wasn't looking directly at them.

The lights, too, were strange. Every time she flicked the switch, they would flicker, dim, then brighten again—flickering in time with the whispers that seemed to come from the walls. It was as if the house itself was breathing, the air thick with its presence. Even when she tried to dismiss it as nothing more than her imagination running wild after everything that had happened, the feeling never left. The house was still watching her.

Lamia's family stayed by her side, trying to comfort her. Her aunt would sit at her bedside, patting her hand gently, trying to reassure her that everything would be fine. But Lamia could see it in her eyes—the unease, the confusion, the quiet fear that her aunt wasn't telling her everything. There was something more to this, something they weren't saying. Every time Lamia would ask about what happened—about the time she'd been unconscious—her aunt would look away, her lips pressed tightly together, as if trying to keep a secret that was eating away at her.

In the mornings, the house was eerily silent. No sounds of birds, no rustling leaves. The air outside felt still, heavy with an oppressive sense of waiting. The walls of the house seemed to close in around Lamia as she moved through the hallways, the creaking of the wooden floors beneath her feet too loud, too ominous.

She would walk into a room and pause, feeling as though the walls were closing in, watching her, judging her. She couldn't shake the feeling that there were eyes on her, even when no one was around. The house seemed to know when she was alone, when she was weak, and it would draw her in deeper.

One evening, after a particularly unsettling moment in the mirror, Lamia tried to escape the feeling by heading outside for a walk. The air was thick with fog, the kind that made it hard to see more than a few steps ahead. The fog felt like a shroud, covering the world in a thick, oppressive blanket. She could barely hear her own footsteps over the sound of her heartbeat thudding in her ears.

But as she walked, something caught her eye—a shadow darting between the trees in the distance. Lamia froze. She wasn't alone.

She turned and hurried back inside, locking the door behind her, but even then, the feeling didn't go away. It was in the air, thick and suffocating, and Lamia couldn't shake the sense that the house was still there, following her, pulling her back into its grip.

That night, as she lay in bed, the whispers returned. They were faint at first, barely audible, but soon they grew louder. Lamia... Lamia... Her name echoed through the walls, a soft and twisted sound, as though the house itself was calling her.

She tried to ignore it, to drown it out, but the more she tried, the louder it became. The house wasn't just watching her—it was trying to speak to her, to claim her once again.

The next morning, Lamia awoke with a start. The room was quiet—too quiet—and for a moment, she thought she was alone. But when she looked into the mirror across the room, she saw her reflection. Or rather, she saw part of it. The other part was... gone. It was as though the reflection had split in two, one side standing still while the other moved on its own, twisting, changing, forming into something else.

A familiar face—the hollow-eyed figure—stared back at her, grinning. It wasn't her reflection anymore. It was something else entirely.

And just as quickly, the reflection disappeared, leaving Lamia standing there, staring at the empty glass.

Her heart pounded in her chest, and she stumbled back from the mirror. It was real. It was all real. The house was still there. The whispers were real. And Lamia was still trapped, caught between two worlds, neither of which she truly belonged to.

The house was watching her. It would never let her go.

4o mini

The Mirror's Revelation

One cold evening, as the dim light from the bedside lamp flickered in the corner of her room, Lamia noticed something unusual. There, resting on her bedside table, was an old photo—one she had never seen before. Her hand shook as she picked it up, her heart pounding with a strange sense of dread. The image was of her as a young child, no more than five or six, standing in front of Hollow Manor. Her eyes were wide with innocent wonder, her small hand outstretched as though she were reaching for something just beyond her grasp.

But the more Lamia stared at the photo, the more she realized that there was something deeply unsettling about it. The house behind her was not just a house. It was alive in the photo. The windows seemed to glimmer with a strange light, and the shadows around it stretched, as if the house itself were watching her, even back then.

Suddenly, the memory struck her like a wave crashing against the shore. The memories of her childhood that she had buried deep inside came rushing back in a flood of vivid images—tales her aunt had whispered to her, stories about the house that she had never fully understood. She remembered the strange feeling of being drawn to Hollow Manor, even as a small child, and how it had called to her—beckoning her, drawing her closer.

But she had escaped, hadn't she?

She could recall the last moments of her time there, the dark halls of the house fading behind her as she ran, heart racing, out into the daylight. She had thought she had made it out, that she had escaped the mansion's dark grip once and for all. But the photo in her hand, the eerie shadows, and the haunting memories all told a different story.

The house had let her go.

It had let her think she was free.

The weight of this realization settled heavily on Lamia's chest. The house had never truly released her—it had simply waited, patiently, allowing her to believe that she was safe, that she had escaped its clutches. But the house was always watching. It had been with her all along, hiding in the corners of her mind, whispering through the cracks in her thoughts, waiting for the moment when it would claim her again.

Her hand trembled as she set the photo down. Her reflection caught her eye in the mirror across the room. But this time, it wasn't just her reflection.

The hollow-eyed figure appeared again, its cold, lifeless eyes staring back at her. Its smile twisted, stretching impossibly wide, as if it were trying to escape from the glass.

Lamia staggered back, her breath coming in short gasps. She could feel the house's presence more than ever before.

It was as if the walls themselves were closing in on her, the air growing thick and oppressive. Her skin crawled, and she could hear the whispers again, the voices growing louder, echoing in her ears.

Lamia... you can't hide. You never really left.

The words echoed in her mind, chilling her to the bone. Her heart raced as the house's grip on her tightened once again. There was no escape. Not now. Not ever. The house had claimed her long ago, and no matter how far she ran, it would always find a way to bring her back.

But she couldn't give up. Not yet.

Lamia turned back to the mirror, staring into the depths of the glass. The reflection stared back at her—no, not her—the hollow-eyed figure that had haunted her dreams, that had been with her all this time, grinning in the darkness.

With a shudder, Lamia reached out and touched the glass.

The instant her fingers brushed against the surface, the mirror seemed to ripple. The room around her shifted, distorting, stretching, pulling her in. The air was thick, heavy with the weight of something ancient and powerful. The house had finally taken hold of her, and the truth was undeniable now.

She had never escaped.

The whispers grew louder, more frantic. The shadows from the corners of the room twisted and danced, filling the space around her. The house was alive, and it had been waiting for her all along.

She was back. She was home.

And no matter how hard she fought, she would never truly be free. The house had her now—body and soul.

The Final Reflection

Lamia, born from the darkness of Hollow Manor, has been waiting. For centuries, she has stood in the shadows of her crumbling home, watching the world pass by, knowing that no one dares to enter. The manor, once a grand palace, is now little more than a decaying husk, its walls covered in moss, its floors warped and broken, but Lamia remains, as eternal as the darkness itself.

The manor is a place of illusions. It is a world of false realities, where nothing is as it seems. When she lures her victims in, she does not offer them promises of riches or power. She does not speak of comfort or warmth, for those are not what they need. Instead, she offers them a glimpse into a reality that they desire, a world where their deepest wishes can come true. It is an illusion, of course—one carefully crafted by Lamia herself.

The children who stumble upon Hollow Manor are always lost. They have no idea that they are walking into a trap, drawn by the whispers of promises that are too good to be true. The manor calls to them in the dead of night, pulling them away from their homes, away from the safety of their families, into its darkened halls. Once inside, they are lost, swept into the maze of mirrors that reflect not what they are, but what they fear most. Every step they take leads them further into Lamia's domain, deeper into the web of illusions she has spun for them.

Lamia watches them from the shadows, waiting for the perfect moment to strike. She knows their fears, their desires, their weaknesses. She feeds on them, not by devouring their flesh, but by consuming their very essence, their innocence, and their souls. The manor, though old and broken, is alive with the energy of the souls she has trapped within its walls. They are her power, her sustenance, her reason for existence.

The mirrors in the manor are not mere reflections. They are windows into other worlds—worlds of the mind, where every thought, every fear, every desire is magnified a thousand times. Lamia has learned to bend these mirrors to her will. She does not need to speak to lure her victims closer; the mirrors do the work for her. They show her victims what they most want to see: a mother's loving smile, a father's embrace, a world free from pain and suffering. And as they step closer to the mirrors, they find themselves pulled deeper into Lamia's illusion.

But there is a twist. The more they look, the more they are drawn in, the more the illusion distorts. What they thought was a safe place becomes their worst nightmare. The reflection of their loved ones twists into grotesque figures, their faces contorted in agony, their eyes filled with terror. The comforting world they once believed in shatters, replaced by a nightmare that they cannot escape.

Lamia stands at the heart of the manor, her eyes never leaving the mirrors. She is not just a queen, not just a monster. She is the embodiment of fear itself, the darkness that lurks at the edges of every mind. She has no need for weapons, no need for tricks—she is the terror that dwells in the deepest corners of the human soul. She is what happens when fear becomes flesh.

As she gazes into one of the mirrors, she sees herself. Not the woman she once was, not the beautiful, proud queen who ruled over a kingdom. No, the woman in the mirror is something far worse. She is a creature of shadows and despair, her face pale and gaunt, her eyes dark pools that seem to suck in the very light around her. Her skin is ashen, cracked like the walls of Hollow Manor, and her hair is a tangled mass of blackness that twists and writhes like a living thing.

This is the reflection she has become. This is the monster she has turned into.

And yet, as she stares into her own reflection, she feels something stir within her—a fleeting sense of recognition, a reminder of the woman she once was. The queen. The ruler. The one who had everything. She had been beautiful, powerful, loved. And now she is nothing but a shadow, a reflection of her own worst fears.

Lamia knows that this is the curse she must live with. She has no choice but to wait, to remain trapped within the illusions she has created. The mirror is her prison, and she is both its warden and its prisoner. But there is one thing she has learned over the centuries: time means nothing here. The manor, the mirrors, the darkness—these are all eternal. And as long as they exist, Lamia will exist too.

But even as she stands there, watching her reflection twist and change, something shifts within her. She is not just a character in a story. She is not just a monster created by fear. She is more than that. She is the embodiment of every fear, every doubt, every darkness that lurks within the hearts of those who look into the mirror.

Lamia is the mirror itself. She is the reflection that cannot be escaped. She is the thing that waits just behind the glass, the part of the mind that no one ever wants to face.

And as she waits in the shadows of Hollow Manor, she knows that it is only a matter of time before someone else comes. Someone else who will wander into the manor, lost and confused, seeking solace in the illusions Lamia has crafted for them. They will stand before the mirror, and when they do, they will see what Lamia has become. They will see their own darkest fears reflected back at them.

The moment they step into the manor, they will be trapped, just as she was. The illusions will pull them in, leading them deeper into the maze of mirrors and shadows. And when they find themselves standing before the mirror, they will realize too late that there is no escape. There is no way to run, no way to hide. The mirror will reflect their deepest, darkest fears, and they will be consumed by them, just as Lamia was.

Lamia has been waiting for this moment for centuries. She knows it will come. She knows that the next victim, the next lost soul, will soon stand before her mirror, just as she once did.

And when that moment comes, she will be ready. The illusion will be perfect. The reflection will be too powerful to resist.

And when they try to escape, when they run, they will find that the mirror is always there, waiting, watching. They will never be able to escape.

So, the next time you see a thing or two off about your reflection, or something just around the corner of your eye when you see the mirror, remember- it might not "just be your imagination" it could be Lamia out there trying to get you.

You will know that you are already lost.

Why Lamia?

Now if you are wondering why the name Lamia, in Greek mythology, Lamia was a beautiful queen who, after a series of tragic events caused by jealousy, was transformed into a monster, roaming the earth in search of children to capture. And so because this Lamia in the story also had a same character as the Lamia in mythology, this would be the perfect name

Mirror Staring Illusion

The **Mirror Staring Illusion** happens when you look at your reflection in dim light for a while. Strange things can start to happen:

What Happens

People often see their own face begin to change. They might see distorted features, like a creepy smile or dark eyes. Some might even see other faces—like monsters, animals, or even people they know who have passed away.

How It Happens

The changes can be small, like shifts in color or shadow, but sometimes the face appears twisted or transformed. The dim light and extended staring seem to "trick" the brain.

Why It Happens

When we look at faces—our own or others'—our brain processes what we see using similar mechanisms. In low light, our brain struggles to make sense of the image and begins to "fill in" the gaps, creating these eerie or unfamiliar effects. This is why we sometimes "see" faces that aren't really there.

My Biography

Hi, I'm Indu Dixit, and I'm 12 years old. I've published 4 books so far (including this one), and I'm really proud of it! I started writing when I was in 1st grade and wrote my first story just for fun. A few months ago, I ended up publishing it, which was a big deal for me. I even gave a speech about it in school.

All my books include-

- Ava's new pet
- Exoplanetary Viability Check
- The Hollow Eyes
- And this one